FANTASTIC MR. FOX

by Roald Dahl

PUFFIN BOOKS
An Imprint of Penguin Group (USA) Inc.

PUFFIN BOOKS
Published by the Penguin Group: London, New York, Australia, Canada, India, Ireland, New Zealand, and South Africa
Penguin Books Ltd, Registered Offices: 80 Strand, London WC2R 0RL, England

First published in the United States of America by Puffin Books, a division of Penguin Young Readers Group, 2009

1 3 5 7 9 10 8 6 4 2

Printed in Mexico

Puffin Books ISBN: 978-0-14-241454-5

Down in the valley there were three farms.
The owners of these farms had done well. They were
rich men. They were also nasty men. Their names
were Farmer *Boggis*, Farmer **Bunce** and Farmer BEAN.

Boggis was a chicken farmer.
He was **ENORMOUSLY** fat.

Bunce was a duck-and-goose farmer.
He was a kind of pot-bellied dwarf.

BEAN was a turkey-and-apple farmer.
He was as **thin** as a pencil
and the cleverest of them all.

> *"Boggis and Bunce and Bean*
> *One fat, one short, one lean.*
> *These horrible crooks*
> *So different in looks*
> *Were none the less equally mean."*

That is what the children used to sing
when they saw them.

MR. FOX

On a hill above the valley there was a wood.
In the wood there was a huge tree.
Under the tree there was a hole.
In the hole lived **Mr. Fox** and **Mrs. Fox**
and their **Small Foxes.**

Every evening as soon as it got dark, **Mr. Fox** would say to **Mrs. Fox**, "Well, my darling, what shall it be this time?

A plump chicken from *Boggis*?
A duck or a goose from **Bunce**?
Or a nice turkey from Bean?"

And when **Mrs. Fox** had told him what she wanted, **Mr. Fox** would creep down into the valley in the darkness of the night and help himself.

Boggis and **Bunce** and Bean knew very well what was going on, and it made them wild with rage.

"Dang and blast that lousy beast!" cried *Boggis*.

"I'd like to rip his guts out!" said **Bunce**.

Bean picked his nose delicately with a long finger. "I have a plan," he said. "Tomorrow night we will all hide just outside the hole where the fox lives. We will wait there until he comes out. Then . . .

Bang! Bang-bang-bang."

The Shooting

"Now do be careful," said **Mrs. Fox**.

"Don't you worry about me," said **Mr. Fox**.

Mr. Fox crept up the dark tunnel to the mouth of his hole. He poked his long handsome face out into the night air and sniffed once.

His black nose twitched from side to side, sniffing for the scent of danger.

He crept a little further out of the hole . . . then further still.

Just then, his sharp night-eyes caught a glint of something bright. It was a small silver speck of moonlight shining on a polished surface. **Mr. Fox** lay still, watching it.

What on earth was it?

. . . Great heavens! It was the barrel of a gun!

Bang-bang! Bang-bang! Bang-bang!

The smoke from the three guns floated upward in the night air. "Did we get him?" said BEAN.

There on the ground lay the poor tattered bloodstained remains of . . . a fox's tail.

"I reckon there's a whole family of them down that hole," **Bunce** said.

"Then we'll have the lot," said BEAN. "Get the shovels!"

THE TERRIBLE SHOVELS

"It hurts," said **Mr. Fox**. "I shall be tail-less for the rest of my life." He looked very glum.

There was no food that night. **Mr. Fox** couldn't sleep because of the pain in the stump of his tail. "Well," he thought, "and now they've found our hole, we're going to have to move out as soon as possible. We'll never get any peace if we . . . What was *that*?"

He turned his head sharply and listened. "Wake up!" he shouted. "They're digging us out!"

Scrunch, scrunch, scrunch.

Suddenly the sharp end of a shovel came right through the ceiling. "There's not a moment to lose!" shouted **Mr. Fox**, beginning to dig. "Nobody in the world can dig as quick as a fox!"

Mrs. **Fox** ran forward to help him. Their front legs were moving so fast you couldn't see them. And gradually the **scrunching** and **scraping** of the shovels became fainter and fainter.

"Phew!" said **Mr. Fox**. "I think we've done it!"

They all sat down, panting for breath. And **Mrs. Fox** said to her children, "Your father is a FANTASTIC FOX."

Mr. Fox looked at his wife and she smiled. He loved her more than ever when she said things like that.

As the sun rose the next morning, *Boggis* and **Bunce** and Bean were still digging. They had dug a hole so deep you could have put a house into it. But they had not yet come to the end of the foxes' tunnel. Bean rubbed the back of his neck. "What we need on this job," he said, "is mechanical shovels."

THE TERRIBLE TRACTORS

The machines went to work, biting huge mouthfuls of soil out of the hill. Down in the tunnel the foxes crouched, listening to the terrible clanging and banging overhead.

"Tractors!" shouted Mr. Fox. "And mechanical shovels! Dig for your lives!

Dig, dig, dig!"

"Keep going!" the fat *Boggis* shouted to **Bunce** and Bean. "We'll get him any moment now!"

The hole the machines had dug was like the crater of a volcano. Bean's face was purple with rage. **Bunce** was cursing the fox with dirty words that cannot be mentioned. *Boggis* said, "What the heck do we do now?"

"I'll tell you what we *don't* do," Bean said. "We don't let him go! We starve him out. We camp here day and night watching the hole. He'll come out in the end. He'll have to."

Fox Has a Plan

Every so often, **Mr. Fox** would creep a little closer towards the mouth of the tunnel and take a sniff. Then he would creep back again and say, "They're still there."

"Are you quite sure?" **Mrs. Fox** would ask.

"Positive," said **Mr. Fox**. "I can smell that man BEAN a mile away. He stinks."

For three days and three nights this waiting-game went on. Down in the tunnel the foxes were slowly but surely starving to death.

Mr. Fox had not spoken for a long time. **Mrs. Fox** knew that he was trying desperately to think of a way out.

"I've just had a bit of an idea. This time we must go in a very special direction," said **Mr. Fox**, pointing sideways and downward.

So he and his children started to dig once again. The work went much more slowly now. Yet little by little the tunnel began to grow.

At last **Mr. Fox** gave the order to stop. "I think," he said, "we had better take a peep upstairs now and see where we are."

Slowly, wearily, the foxes began to slope the tunnel up towards the surface.
"Unless I am very much mistaken, we are right underneath somebody's house," whispered **Mr. Fox**. "Be very quiet now."
Carefully, **Mr. Fox** began pushing up one of the floorboards. He let out a shriek of excitement.

Boggis's Chicken House

"I've done it!" he yelled, and started prancing and dancing with joy. "Come on up!" he sang out. "What a sight for a hungry fox!"

And what a fantastic sight it was that now met their eyes! There were white chickens and brown chickens and black chickens by the thousand!

"*Boggis's Chicken House Number One*!" cried **Mr. Fox**. "It's exactly what I was aiming at!"

Mr. Fox chose three of the plumpest hens. "Back to the tunnel!" he ordered. "Come on! No fooling around! The quicker you move, the quicker you shall have something to eat!"

They climbed down through the hole in the floor. **Mr. Fox** reached up and pulled the floorboards back into place. He did it so that no one could tell they had ever been moved.

"My son," he said, giving the plump hens to one of his Small Foxes, "run back with these to your mother. Tell her to prepare a feast. The rest of us will be along in a jiffy, as soon as we have made a few other little arrangements.

"Now for the next bit, my darlings! This one'll be as easy as pie! All we have to do is dig another little tunnel from here to there!

Start digging!"

BADGER

All of a sudden a deep voice above their heads said, *"Who goes there?"* The foxes jumped.

"Badger!" cried **Mr. Fox**.

"Foxy!" cried Badger. "My goodness me! None of us can get out! We're all starving to death!"

"My dear old Badger, this mess you're in is all my fault . . ."

"I *know* it's your fault!" said Badger furiously. "And the farmers are not going to give up till they've got you. My poor wife up there is so weak she can't dig another yard."

"Nor can mine," said **Mr. Fox**. "And yet at this very minute she is preparing the most delicious feast of plump juicy chickens . . . And because everything is entirely my fault, I invite you to share the feast. I invite *everyone* to share it. There'll be plenty to go round."

"You mean it?" cried Badger.

"Yes! You can help us dig."

Badger was a great digger and the tunnel went forward at a terrific pace now that he was lending a paw.

BUNCE'S MIGHTY STOREHOUSE

Soon they were crouching underneath yet another wooden floor. **Mr. Fox** grinned slyly, showing sharp white teeth. "If I am not mistaken, my dear Badger," he said, "we are now underneath the farm which belongs to that nasty little pot-bellied dwarf, **Bunce**." He pushed up one wooden floorboard, then another. "This, my dear old Badger," proclaimed **Mr. Fox**, "is **Bunce's Mighty Storehouse**!" **Mr. Fox** began prowling around the storehouse, examining the glorious display with an expert eye. "We mustn't give the game away. We must be neat and tidy and take just a few of the choicest morsels."

Back in the tunnel, **Mr. Fox** again pulled the floorboards very carefully into place so that no one could see they had been moved.

"Just one more visit!" cried **Mr. Fox**.

Badger said, "Doesn't this worry you just a tiny bit, Foxy?"

"Worry me?" said **Mr. Fox**.

"All this . . . this *stealing*."

"My dear old furry frump," he said, "do you know anyone in the *whole world* who wouldn't swipe a few chickens if his children were starving to death? Now let's get on with the digging."

Five minutes later, Badger's front paws hit against something flat and hard. A wall was right in front of them, blocking their way.

Mr. Fox examined the wall carefully. He saw that the cement between the bricks was old and crumbly, so he loosened a brick without much trouble and pulled it away. Suddenly, out from the hole where the brick had been, there popped a small sharp face with whiskers.

"Go away!" it snapped.

"Good Lord!" said Badger. "It's Rat!"

"Go away!" shrieked Rat. "Go on, beat it!"

"Shut up," said Mr. Fox.

"I will not shut up!" shrieked Rat.

Mr. Fox gave a brilliant smile.

"My dear Rat," he said softly, "I am a hungry fellow and if you don't hop it quickly I shall eat-you-up-in-one-gulp!"

Badger peered into the half-darkness. They began to see what looked like a whole lot of big glass jars standing upon shelves around the walls. There were hundreds of them, and upon each one was written the word CIDER.

"Tremendous!" shouted Badger.

"Bean's Cider Cellar," said **Mr. Fox**.

"Cider," said Badger, "is especially good for Badgers. We take it as a medicine —one large glass three times a day with meals and another at bedtime."

"You're poaching!" shrieked Rat. "There'll be none left for me!"

Mr. Fox and Badger ran across the cellar clutching a gallon jar each. "Goodbye, Rat!" they called out as they disappeared through the hole in the wall. "Thanks for the lovely cider!"

The Great Feast

Back in the tunnel they paused so that **Mr. Fox** could brick up the hole in the wall. "There we are. Now, home to the feast!"

Along the tunnel they flew . . .

past the turning that led to **Bunce's Mighty Storehouse** . . .

past *Boggis's Chicken House Number One* . . . and then up the long home stretch towards where they knew **Mrs. Fox** would be waiting.

They rounded the final corner and burst in upon the most wonderful and amazing sight any of them had ever seen.

A large dining-room had been hollowed out of the earth. The table was covered with chickens and ducks and geese and hams and bacon, and everyone was tucking into the lovely food.

"My darling!" cried **Mrs. Fox**, jumping up and hugging **Mr. Fox**. Amid shouts of joy, the great jars of cider were placed upon the table, and **Mr. Fox** and Badger sat down with the others.

You must remember no one had eaten for several days.

They were ravenous. So for a while there was no conversation at all. There was only the sound of **crunching** and *chewing*.

At last, Badger stood up. He raised his glass of cider. "A toast! I want you all to stand and drink a toast to our dear friend who has saved our lives this day—Mr. Fox!"

"To Mr. Fox!" they all shouted, standing up and raising their glasses.

Then Mrs. Fox got shyly to her feet and said, "I just want to say one thing, and it is this: MY HUSBAND IS A FANTASTIC FOX!" Everyone clapped and cheered.

hen **Mr. Fox** himself stood up.

"Let us be serious. Let us think of tomorrow and the next day and the days after that. If we go out, we will be killed. Right?"

"Right!" they shouted.

"Ex-*actly*," said **Mr. Fox**. "But who *wants* to go out anyway? The outside is full of enemies. We only go out because we have to, to get food for our families. But now, my friends, we have a safe tunnel leading to three of the finest stores in the world!"

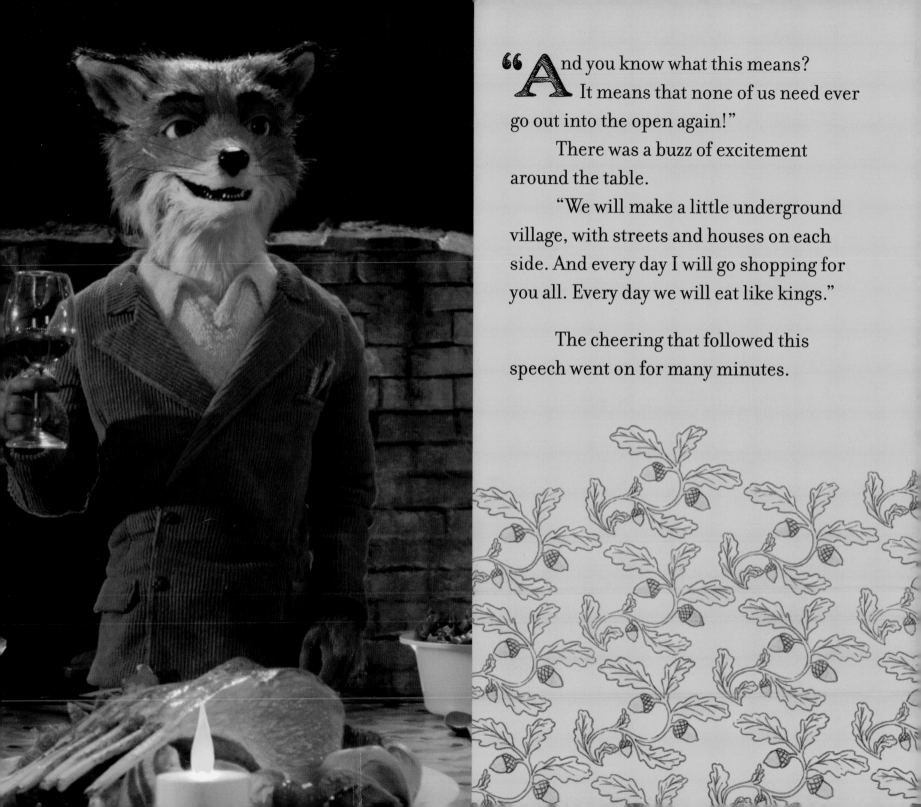

"**A**nd you know what this means? It means that none of us need ever go out into the open again!"

There was a buzz of excitement around the table.

"We will make a little underground village, with streets and houses on each side. And every day I will go shopping for you all. Every day we will eat like kings."

The cheering that followed this speech went on for many minutes.

Outside the fox's hole, *Boggis* and **Bunce** and Bean sat with their guns on their laps.

It was beginning to rain.

"He won't stay down there much longer now," *Boggis* said.

"The brute must be famished," **Bunce** said.

"That's right," Bean said. "He'll be making a dash for it any moment. Keep your guns handy."

They sat there by the hole, waiting for the fox to come out.

And so far as I know, they are **still** waiting.